CASANDRA MERRITT

FROM THE *heart*
OF A COUNSELOR

hey, women... let's talk about it

From the Heart of a Counselor

Published by New Beginnings Publications
www.arisewithcasandra.com

Book Creation and Design
DHBonner Virtual Solutions, LLC
www.dhbonner.net

ISBN: 978-1-7379628-2-3

Printed in the United States of America

Dedicated to my daughters, *Alexandra* and *Myesha*...
Ladies, I love you both so much and pray that you will
always reflect on God's Love for you!

CASANDRA MERRITT

FROM THE *heart*
OF A COUNSELOR

hey, women... let's talk about it

Table of Contents

Acknowledgments

I am incredibly grateful for all the women in my life who have encouraged me to know *My Worth* and *Love Myself.*

I want to thank my husband, Melvin, and our sons. I encourage you to love your wives like Christ loves the church.

Thank you to the **Start Fresh** team. I love and know you are appreciated. I will be forever grateful for the journey.

Introduction

I f you're a woman, this book is for you (although it wouldn't hurt a man to read it)! There are struggles and patterns that seem to settle onto women and affect us in unique ways. As a Christian and mental health counselor and pastor, I feel God has given me an assignment to help women navigate their struggles in life. One way I do this is by enlightening and empowering them to understand their worth and embrace the fact that it is rooted in unconditional love. When they understand that this love is found in Christ alone, a shift in the right direction begins to take place, and they are changed. I know this firsthand because it happened to me many years ago.

From the Heart of a Counselor will highlight some common issues you may find yourself struggling with. Often those who come meet with me say things like, "I don't know what I'm called to do," or "Things never seem to change." These statements are invitations for me to speak biblical and therapeutic truth and help the women I meet with to discover who God is within them and who he has called them to be. They don't have to fall into the same old patterns and cycles they've been stuck in, and neither do you. You don't have to give up your worth . . . ever. Each one of us is an emotional, physical, mental, and spiritual being, and God is for us in all these areas! I've seen him use the wisdom and knowledge of therapy along with the guidance of the Holy Spirit to lead women into healing and redemption time and time again.

Since I may never be able to personally meet with you in my office, I've put some key truths in this book with the hope that they will help you begin to uncover the truths regarding the unconditional love God has for you along with your true potential, leading you to a life worth celebrating.

So, hey, women! Let's get started. Let's talk about these things! I'll begin by identifying who you are...

You are Called, Woman!

Perhaps people have not always treated you as you deserve. Maybe you've questioned your worth, and you are unsure of your calling. Or you're just a little insecure about your identity. You wonder, "Who am I?" and "What does it really mean to be a woman?" Those are great questions and the perfect starting point. So, let's begin by diving into the truth about who you are. Knowing this and taking it to heart will give you a firm foundation and help you in the course of your whole life!

We're given a dictionary definition that tells us simply that a woman is "an adult female human being." But there is a biblical definition of woman that plays out in the Scriptures in both the Old and the New Testaments, which gives us a richer, fuller picture of not only *what* a woman is but *who* she truly is.

Since this definition is given to us by the Creator of life—and specifically, the Creator of women—it seems wise to pay attention to what he has to say, don't you think? God's Word tells us:

"Then the Lord God made a woman from the rib, and he brought her to the man. 'At last!' the man exclaimed. 'This one is bone from my bone and flesh from my flesh! She will be called 'woman' because she was taken from 'man.' This explains why a man leaves his father and mother and is joined to his wife, and the two are united into one" (Genesis 2:22–24).

What a beautiful picture! The woman God made was a special gift, and Adam received her as God intended, with enthusiasm and reverence. "Woman" is a name to be revered.

Later in the next chapter, after some time had passed, Eve was visited by Satan in the form of a serpent, and she was deceived by him. Then, both she and her husband, Adam, disobeyed God and ate from the Tree of the Knowledge of Good and Evil. Following this tragedy, Adam gave his wife her name: "Then the man—Adam—named his wife Eve because she would be the mother of all who live" (Genesis 3:20). The name "Eve" in Hebrew means "life." Even though she made a mistake, Eve was given the honor of being a life-giver.

As a woman, you are a direct descendent of Eve! And the punishments God gave to her were passed down to you. You inherited them. When she (along with Adam) was banished from the Garden of Eden, God said he would multiply her pain during childbirth, and that is certainly our reality today. We're told that Eve's desire and longing would be for her husband, and he would rule [with authority] over her and be responsible for her (Genesis chapter 3, AMP).

Yet, along with the consequences of her sin, you were also given Eve's blessing. As a woman, you, too, are a life-giver—not through motherhood but in your relationships. Even in her sin, God took care of Eve and was with her. He created her from man and presented her back to man. From birth to presentation and beyond, God was with Eve and had a plan for her life.

When God looks at you, dear woman, he sees you as something precious with an important purpose in life. Because he made you, you are valuable and worthy. He made man (and that includes woman) "in his own image," according to Genesis 1:27, and you just have to know he wouldn't make junk! God's Word also tells us to celebrate *how* God made us:

> "I will give thanks and praise to You, for I am fearfully and wonderfully made; Wonderful are Your works, and my soul knows it very well" (Psalm 139:14, NIV).

This truth of you being created by a loving God should define you as a person, and if you were born female, it defines you as a woman. God took Eve out of man and then presented her to man. She was a special gift to Adam as you are a gift to your husband if you are married, and if not, you are special, But God didn't intend just for Eve to be for Adam. Adam was also for Eve. God gives gifts of relationships (through friendships, marriage, and family) for you as well. You would be wise to navigate those relationships with your Creator's guidance as you keep in mind how he made you: fearfully (a synonym for this is "extraordinarily") and wonderfully.

You are precious in his sight. Valuable.

So, if you are in a relationship or thinking about getting involved in one with someone who doesn't value you, then recognize that it is less than God's best for you. Don't cheapen yourself by settling for it. Don't give away your worth like that! (I will highlight this truth throughout this book because it is so foundationally important.) Wait for God's intended gift to come your way and save yourself a lot of heartache, pain, drama, and trauma! Do you know God loves you unconditionally? Your self-worth is tied to that fact if you accept it.

If you don't know the truth of God's love—that it is unconditional and ever-present—then you won't be able to fully grasp how valuable you are, and you will settle for relationships that are not good for you. When you do understand and accept that your Creator took great care in making you and made you out of his unconditional love, you will celebrate the truth of who you are as a woman and your true worth as a woman. Then, you will be secure in who you are and more able to invite the right relationships into your life.

I hope you now have a clearer picture of who you are as a woman. God created and loved Eve (even in her disobedience toward him), and he created and loves you—no matter your sin and mistakes. Of course, none of us started out as women as Eve did—fashioned out of a rib bone! We grow into our "position" of being a woman. Much of becoming a woman is not so much determined by our physicality or by our age but by our emotional intelligence. And much of that is determined by the severity and types of tragedy we have suffered in life and how those things have been or are being processed.

Your goal in your womanhood should be to mature and live out of a place of spiritual and emotional health. In order to do that, you must reconcile your past with your present.

The Loss of Protection

As a counselor, I meet with a lot of female clients who do not grasp or believe their true value. Often they have a distorted view of their worth and of who God made them to be as women. As a result, they make poor choices as to *whom* they allow into their lives (specifically men) and—intentionally or unintentionally—*what* they allow into their lives.

More often than not, this can be traced back to a lack of protection in their life at an early age, primarily by a loving and present father, though it's not limited to that.

When we're protected, it means we are sheltered, guarded, and preserved; it means we are in safe hands and can feel secure. As children, we look to our parents for that care, as we should. Naturally, that's our first earthly encounter or experience with protection. When we are not protected, we are vulnerable to all sorts of pain and dysfunction.

I experienced a lack of protection in my early life. I never knew my father. My mother was only twelve years old when she conceived me out of rape. I was put into a children's home for a time, and then my maternal grandmother raised me until my senior year of high school, when she passed away from cancer. I was once married to a man I barely knew; I agreed to marry him because I was looking and longing for stability.

I already had a son out of wedlock, and I knew I didn't want more kids without being married. I was struggling as a single mom and with life in general. I was in college and working, and I felt desperate to get away from my environment. I longed to experience unconditional love and to be cherished and cared for, so I entered into marriage with the hope that it would give me a better life. Unfortunately, the marriage became abusive, and I suffered from his verbal and physical abuse. I discovered later that he experienced some mental health issues.

I reveal (in brief) this part of my life to illustrate the all-too-familiar outcome of the missing piece beginning the day of my conception: I did not have a father. I didn't have a male figure who recognized that I was bone of his bone, flesh of his flesh, and something to be valued and guarded. I had no covering from him, and therefore, I suffered a loss of protection in my early life. Let me be clear; this doesn't mean God was absent as I can look back and see many ways he protected me, but I was still greatly affected by my earthly parents' lack of protective care, which left an opening for the enemy (yes, Satan is real, and he is our enemy) to do what he wanted to do.

Satan went on the attack. He deceived me over the years, and I developed dangerous patterns and ways of thinking.

I'm not saying I didn't have a choice. I definitely did, and so do you. No matter what has taken place in our lives due to the sin of omission or the sin of commission. (These are sins that either we do, or someone does against us. Regarding ourselves, the *omission* is something that we have failed to do, and *commission* is something we have done.) You see, we can't solely blame Satan or people for our choices, but we can understand why we may tend to make poor choices and fail to do what we need to in order to protect ourselves. It's like us having a home full of valuables and leaving the front door unlocked, the windows open, and turning the alarm system off. If we do nothing to keep our home safe, then we can be sure that at some point, an intruder will break in and steal from us because we've left things unprotected!

We, as women, are valuable property. God designed us to be protected by our earthly parents, but sometimes they are not around, and they fail us. When that happens, and as we get older, we must be aware of our vulnerabilities brought on by our past and make the right choices to protect ourselves in our present and in the future. You may have had a loving and fully-present parents, and yet harm still occurred. That's because we live in a sin-contaminated world.

Satan loves to wreak havoc and promote dysfunction. He's all about loss and doesn't want us to experience protection. The Bible calls him a "thief" and tells us he " . . . comes only in order to steal and kill and destroy" (John 10:10, AMP), and he had a heyday with me. Thankfully, however, that's not the end of my story, and if you've lived a similar experience, it's not the end of your story either. God surely did protect me along the way, but I didn't understand the power of the eternal protection I have in him until I accepted Christ as my Savior. When I invited Christ in, he reversed the curse of my loss of protection. I had to repent of the sin that plagued my life—my own sin and the sins that were committed against me, and the known sins of the generations before me. Doing this breaks cycles and frees us from strongholds. The "Fall of Man," which is what we call Adam and Eve's disobedience, caused contamination in our world. I learned I could not participate in that contamination and that I needed to be saved from it. Sin may feel good at the time we're doing it, and much of the time, it looks good and "normal." Yet, in reality, it is deadly.

The rest of John 10:10 (AMP) goes on to say, "I (Jesus) came that they (you and I) may have and enjoy life and have it in abundance [to the full till it overflows]. That is good and powerful news! That's gospel truth! Once I accepted Jesus as my Lord and Savior, I began to experience restoration, encouragement, insight, and the renewing of my mind. That's when the transformation happened, and I understood who I really was. I understood my worth! From there, I could participate in protecting myself from harmful relationships by making wise and worthy choices. There is hope and restoration for us all in Jesus, no matter the severity of our past. Maybe your situation is different from mine. Maybe you've never been physically abused or experienced poverty or homelessness. Perhaps on the outside, your life appears to be going quite nicely, but secretly you are cutting, taking drugs, drinking too much, or you're engaged privately in other destructive activities. Maybe you're living in anger or fear. Jesus is willing and able to restore you as well. You must address what needs to be dealt with in your life as it separates you from God's wholeness. You will have his protection when you belong to him. You can have this by:

- Recognizing or having an awareness of the sin in your life.
- Repenting of that sin.
- Accepting God's love by inviting Jesus to be your Savior.

In Christ, you are protected! You now have access to him, so call upon his name! That's not to say you won't be a victim sometimes or that you won't make wrong choices, but when you belong to him, you can claim Romans 8:38–39 (AMP):

"For I am convinced [and continue to be convinced—beyond any doubt] that neither death nor life nor angels nor principalities nor things present and threatening nor things to come nor powers nor height nor depth nor any other created thing will be able to separate us from the [unlimited] love of God, which is in Christ Jesus our Lord."

We all want and need unconditional love. Whether you know it or not, that's what you're looking for in a relationship. I'm sorry for the loss of protection you may have experienced in your past, but I want to encourage you to move forward with Jesus and let him help you and love you as you desire and deserve... unconditionally.

Once you accept Christ and make Him your Master, you can be free to think differently and are empowered to abandon your old ways of approaching things. Proverbs 14:12 says, "There is a way that seems to be right, but in the end it leads to death."

I was living in Guam with my first marriage—we were a military family—when I encountered Christ and accepted him. At the time, I was feeling unhappy and desperate. The anger and abuse had been uncovered, and I was experiencing severe anxiety from our life together, which was affecting me physically. I needed help, so I asked him to drive me to a church he knew of on the island. When we arrived, I bolted out of the car, dashed into the church building, and ran down the aisle straight to one of the pastors! Thankfully, the service had not started yet!

She asked if I was alright, and I responded, nearly out of breath, with a bold, "No! I'm not!" She told me to follow her and led me to a mop and broom closet! Inside those four walls, she looked me straight in the eyes and asked, "Do you want to accept Jesus Christ?" I replied, "Well, if it's going to make things better, then yes!" I prayed with her right there in that closet, and it was the best decision I've ever made! I came out of that closet with every ounce of faith that I could muster, believing that the Lord could and would change my situation. And he did! Of course, not all at that moment; however, I immediately experienced his unconditional love, peace, and protection.

This isn't to say my life was suddenly perfect, but I began to see God do things that I never imagined. He protected me and covered me—even in the midst of times of chaos and confusion.

I remained his wife, but after thirteen years of marriage, he ended up giving me a divorce. I realize now, however, that even *that* was God's protection in my life!

When you accept Jesus, you instantly belong to him, and you will live differently and make wiser choices, which will help protect you. You must play your part, however. It's essential that you keep your eyes on Christ. This means don't focus more on your circumstances than you do on him. In him, you will find guidance and strength. Depend on him. Trust him. Have faith, and follow his ways. Then, you will have a better life and experience and recognize his loving protection.

Romans 12:2 (AMP) sums it up nicely:

"And do not be conformed to this world [any longer, with its superficial values and customs], but be transformed and progressively changed [as you mature spiritually] by the renewing of your mind, [focusing on godly values and ethical attitudes] so that you may prove [for yourselves] what the will of God is, that which is good and acceptable and perfect [in His plan and purpose for you]."

The Spirit of Sabotage

Let me ask you something: Are you getting in your own way? Even though you may understand who you are as a woman, are you living out of the fullness of who God made you to be? If you experienced the loss of protection in your past, and you recognize how that caused you to suffer as a child and how it continues to affect you in some form today, are you able to move beyond it and experience healing? The Lord is willing and able to help, but again, we must play our part.

When we don't face and deal with these things head-on, it's all too easy to fall into self-sabotaging behaviors and attitudes. Maybe you're inviting or simply allowing destruction to take place in your life instead of actively fighting against those behaviors and attitudes that are harming you. If so, let me tell you, dear woman, self-sabotage does not have to be your reality.

The essential meaning of *sabotage*, according to the Merriam-Webster Dictionary, is "the act of destroying or damaging something deliberately so that it does not work correctly."

A psychological definition of self-sabotage states:

> Self-sabotage occurs when we destroy ourselves physically, mentally, or emotionally or deliberately hinder our own success and wellbeing by undermining personal goals and values. (Brenner, 2019)

Sometimes, we don't really know that we are destroying ourselves when we go back to negative behaviors and wrong thought processes over and over again, but I challenge you now to take a hard look at these things and be honest with yourself about what they are producing.

Behavior is said to be self-sabotaging when it creates problems in daily life and interferes with long-standing goals. For example, "Someone with a fear of failure might wait until the last minute to work on an important project, unconsciously avoiding the prospect of advancement" (Wignall, 2020).

As a whole, self-sabotage is not tied to one event but to multiple personal choices. At its root are mindsets that are counterproductive, including negativity, disorganization, indecisiveness, and negative self-talk. Though we have the power to make different choices and promote better outcomes for ourselves, often we choose to stay in what seems to be comfortable for us, even when it's destructive.

A major reason why people self-sabotage is that they live with low self-esteem. The cause of a lack of healthy self-esteem in our lives can be many things, but the effects play out in similar ways. When we don't have a right view of ourselves (knowing and believing we are who God says we are), we suffer the effects of low self-esteem, which include feelings of worthlessness or incompetence, the belief that we don't deserve success, and even self-hatred.

One example of physical self-sabotage is not taking care of our own health. Are you neglecting exercise and healthy eating? Are you allowing yourself to be overweight or underweight and not making an effort to be physically healthy? Are you doing all that you can to get a good night's sleep? When you don't feel well physically—due to your own neglect or imbalance—you won't feel well emotionally. You will have a negative mindset and think things like, "I can't do such-and-such," and "I'm not good enough, beautiful enough ... " When your physical self is being ignored, or your thoughts regarding it are distorted, you are self-sabotaging.

Being obsessed with how we look leads to self-sabotage as well. We can also make too much of our outer beauty and try to get our worth from our physical appearance. There is nothing wrong with presenting ourselves well and adorning ourselves with makeup, fashionable clothes, and the like, but we must allow God to direct that part of our life and help us to keep things in balance.

An insightful quote from actress Rosalind Russell says, "Taking joy in living is a woman's best cosmetic."

When this area of our life is out of balance, we neglect the more lasting, important part of who we are. We are wise to put our physical being in God's trust because then he will direct us in this area of how much focus to put on our physical appearance and help protect us from self-sabotage.

Perhaps as you go about your life, you tend to walk along a good path and make positive progress in an area for a while, but then you find yourself back to that familiar place (not necessarily a physical place but a mindset, a habit, a relationship, etc.) that isn't good for you. This pattern may point to a stronghold in your life. Are you in a relationship that you know is not the best for you? Are you engaged in certain behaviors you know are wrong but you can't seem to stop? Are you trying to take the easy way out of something instead of staying on the right path? Are you compromising in some way? Do you live in fear, worry, or despair?

If you see yourself in any of these scenarios (there are countless others), it's likely there is a stronghold in your life, and it's sabotaging you. Old habits and former ways of thinking can become strongholds. Pastor and author Max Lucado refers to strongholds as "old, difficult, discouraging challenges." When they come upon you, and as they play out, it's common to self-isolate and live in shame and feel like others are rejecting you. Satan loves to keep you in that cycle. Recognizing self-sabotaging behaviors and ways of thinking is the first step to putting an end to them.

Actually, you must go a step further and not just recognize them but own them. Then, confess these strongholds that manifest themselves in behavior and get them out of your life!

Once again, no one forces you to make wrong choices. You are a woman made in God's image, and when you have Christ, you have all you need to make the right choices. You have that power!

"I also pray that you will understand the incredible greatness of God's power for us who believe in him. This is the same mighty power that raised Christ from the dead and seated him in the place of honor at God's right hand in the heavenly realms" (Ephesians 1:19–20, NLT).

Remind yourself of the power inside you because of Christ. Also, take to heart these encouraging words from 2 Timothy 1:7 (AMP):

"For God did not give us a spirit of timidity or cowardice or fear, but [He has given us a spirit] of power and of love and of sound judgment and personal discipline, [abilities that result in a calm, well-balanced mind and self-control]."

You see? God has equipped you with the power you need; you just have to put that power into practice.

An enemy of that power can be your own emotions. You must seek to understand the emotions that tend to lead you to make certain choices and engage in familiar negative behavior. Do you recognize them? Can you notice any patterns? When you do, it will help you take control of those emotions before they control you, and you find yourself acting on them in ways that are self-sabotaging.

There's nothing wrong, by the way, with emotions. There's nothing wrong, for example, with being sad. If someone hurts your feelings, it's normal to feel sad, but you then need to deal with that emotion by expressing how you feel in the right way—maybe only to yourself—so that it doesn't take over.

Dealing with sadness in a healthy way releases it and allows you to regain your posture and be able to realign your emotions so that you are able to operate properly again. But, when you allow sadness to forget its place and take over, you can find yourself entering self-sabotage territory! Maybe you struggle to control your anger or feelings of guilt. Perhaps your life is wrought with fear and despair, or feelings of worthlessness paralyze you, and you become "stuck." If you can relate to any of these, you must see them as warning signs. If you need help identifying and dealing with your emotions, I encourage you to meet with a professional counselor who can assist you. There's no shame in needing help! In fact, it's wise and brave to seek it.

While emotions can be controlled, situations are often out of our control. There is nothing we can do to control a situation, but cognitive behavioral therapy teaches us that we have the ability to influence that situation. Stress, for example, will come. It's a part of life. It's not a sin to have stress, but it's a sin to stay in a mindset of stress, and it's destructive in a number of ways. What we have the power to do is deal with both the thoughts that come to us and our belief system. Of course, lots of thoughts come to our brains all at the same time, but the ones that line up with our core beliefs are going to be captured. Our emotions then want to partner with those thoughts that resonate with our belief system.

When that happens, we want to act on them, whether they are positive or negative. When they're positive and healthy—great! But sometimes, they are not. The good news is that we have the power to change our thoughts and beliefs, our emotions, and our behavior. To manage our emotions the best way possible, we must have an encounter with agape love, which is God's unconditional love for us. When we experience agape love, we will continue to have emotions, of course, but they won't get the best of us, and we will better be able to manage them.

In my practice, I've noticed that women tend to want more than anything to first change their situation—even before controlling their emotions—so they spend less time on their "inner self," which is their belief system that controls their emotions, and more effort on trying to manipulate what they can't control! When they fall into this trap, the spirit of sabotage is exhibited. It can manifest itself in overeating, depression, worry, bad temper, bitterness, isolation, etc.

Also, if you choose to involve yourself in wrong actions, like adultery, fornication, taking drugs, and the like, it doesn't matter who you are; self-sabotage will be the result. These types of activities sabotage who you are and who you were created to be. These behaviors and mindsets will keep you from moving forward, being productive, and sticking with your goals. Before you know it, you will be ensnared, and the journey to be set free is always harder than the path you took to get there!

Stay focused on the right path, and choose to keep on it. Don't let self-sabotaging behaviors detour you.

If you slip up, stop. Repent. Let the Lord forgive you, and forgive yourself. Then, get back on the right path, and steer clear of the wrong one. We all make mistakes, but we don't have to continue with them. Encourage yourself to be sustained by the Sustainer—Jesus Christ. Focus on him and his ways, and ask him to help you stay on the path you know he wants for you. God's Word tells us to fix our eyes on Jesus. The Amplified Bible's version of Hebrews 12:2a puts it this way:

> "[looking away from all that will distract us and] focusing our eyes on Jesus, who is the Author and Perfecter of faith [the first incentive for our belief and the One who brings our faith to maturity] . . . "

This means to stare at Jesus; don't just glance at him! Keep your focus on him. This will keep you from getting in your own way and making unwise choices that lead to self-sabotage.

One way to help yourself focus on the Lord and counter self-sabotaging behaviors is to recognize and put an end to any "stinkin' thinkin'" you may be engaged in. You must examine what is in your core belief system. Take a hard look at it because some wrong thinking can be subtle, or you're just so used to it that you don't recognize it. If you don't make the effort to examine your core belief system, then any type of thought is given permission to partner with whatever it has been grounded in.

For instance, if your mother or environment taught you to be critical and think negatively and rarely taught you to think positively or anything encouraging, and you practice this in your own life, you will generally only see the negative side of things. All the "what-ifs" and thoughts of "I just know something bad will happen" will go around and around in your mind and make a mess of you. It will keep you down and keep you from moving forward. You have to put something new in your mind.

To chase off the negative or faulty thinking, meditate (or dwell) on Jesus and who he is and on what's right and good instead of giving your attention to what is wrong and harmful. The Bible is so practical and outlines this clearly in Philippians 4:8, where it says, " . . . whatever is true, whatever is noble, whatever is right, whatever is pure, whatever is lovely, whatever is admirable—if anything is excellent or praiseworthy—think about such things."

These are the types of things you must put into your mind to guard against self-sabotage and harmful or stinkin' thinkin'! And take to heart Romans 12:2 (NLT):

"Don't copy the behavior and customs of this world, but let God transform you into a new person by changing the way you think. Then you will learn to know God's will for you, which is good and pleasing and perfect."

God has such good plans for you, but you need to be careful about how you think and what you think about so you can live out his good and perfect will. Whenever we lose a sense of purpose, we are vulnerable to falling away from anything good—whether it's fellowship with God and other believers, going to school, excelling at work . . . you name it. When we lose our sense of purpose, we aren't trusting God's plan for us, and we sabotage ourselves and our future. So again, stay focused on God's Word.

Also, surround yourself with like-minded, God-thinking people to encourage and help you stay on the right path. I've had at least four strong mentors throughout the years who have fulfilled this role in my life. Some were with me for a season, and they helped me navigate certain challenges I was going through at the time. Others continue mentoring me to this day. We never outgrow the need for someone who has gone before us in life and is willing to walk alongside and mentor us. Seek out one or two people who are more mature in the faith, and ask them to be that in your life. Then, be accountable to them, and listen when they tell you some hard truth.

"Faithful are the wounds of a friend [who corrects out of love and concern], but the kisses of an enemy are deceitful [because they serve his hidden agenda]" (Proverbs 27:6, AMP).

Put these things into practice, and you will be far less likely to be dragged down or revisited by any kind of old self-sabotaging behavior of your past and succumb to it. When you're in Christ and maintain your position, you can combat these temptations and win. Don't be fooled into thinking that you're missing out when you say "no" to the old things. That's a lie from the enemy.

Don't flirt around with your past hurts, desires, etc. Instead, focus on Jesus and listen to the Holy Spirit. He will convict and help you each step of the way.

I'm not saying any of this is easy, but it's doable. Take baby steps, one day at a time. Set a goal for each day. Get up and thank God for breath and life. Then ask him to guide you physically, emotionally, mentally, and spiritually into your day. He is faithful and is for you. You can trust him.

So... now make strides in life with your renewed mind. This is a process, but every step of it will move you forward!

The Cognitive Behavioral Model

Thoughts / Beliefs

What a person thinks or believes about a situation. How the individual interprets an event.

Situation

Anything that happens to a person. Situations are ultimately outside of the individual's control, but they can be influenced by behaviors.

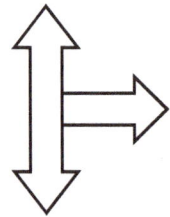

Behavior / Response

The person's actions and behaviors in response to their thoughts and feelings about a situation

Emotions

How a person feels about a situation. Emotions are not necessarily based in logic, but they are influenced by thoughts and beliefs.

Why Am I Freely Giving Away My Worth?

Remind yourself of this truth every day: You were made by God in his image. So, dear woman, you are worth a great deal! By now, you know I appreciate a solid definition, so here's one for *worth* according to Merriam-Webster. Worth is "the value of something measured by its qualities or by the esteem in which it is held."

A woman's worth is the totality of who she is. So, dear woman, you are more than your body. You are more than your age, beauty, and sex appeal! A truly empowered and enlightened woman knows how to love herself and others completely. The Bible tells us, "An excellent woman, [one who is spiritual, capable, intelligent, and virtuous], who is he who can find her? Her value is more precious than jewels, and her worth is far above rubies or pearls" (Proverbs 31:10, AMP).

See? Women are more valuable than some of the most precious items on earth. That's how God made us . . . made you. That's how God sees you, even in your imperfections. When you realize who you are and accept it, you won't give up your worth by your actions or thoughts about yourself. You won't let others devalue you. You'll be able to say, "It's OK that you don't find me beautiful or don't find me worthy of marriage. That just means you're not the one for me!"

How we view ourselves is what makes up our self-esteem. Depending on your self-esteem, you will value or devalue yourself by how you live and how you choose your relationships. I remember being in a relationship years ago that was not good for me, but because I didn't know my worth, I found myself staying with this man much too long. I thought it was okay for me to give myself to this relationship that wasn't prospering and, in reality, wasn't going anywhere. It wasn't genuine. He made me promise after promise that never materialized. Though he gave me the gift of a new ring more than once, the marriage that he said would come with these rings never did.

In the meantime, I continued to give away my worth to him. At that time, I didn't understand my worth as a person and especially as a woman. Finally, I learned I could own my purity, and when I surrendered myself to Christ—my self-image, my beauty, my sexuality, my personhood—I was restored. I was then able to move on from that relationship, and my life improved. Thank God!

When you recognize and embrace your worth as a woman in the right way, not in an arrogant or entitled way, your true beauty shines through. Others will respect your worth as you do. You will move forward in your goals, pursue your dreams, and experience peace with God and others. You won't give away your purity. You will bounce back after setbacks and hardships because they won't define you. You will be comfortable in your own skin. In all this, be careful to never be rude or take on a "mean girl" persona. You can and should still be soft and kind. These attributes are what the Bible calls "imperishable beauty, and they honor your Creator."

1 Peter 3:3–4 (NLT) tells us, "Don't be concerned about the outward beauty of fancy hairstyles, expensive jewelry, or beautiful clothes. You should clothe yourselves instead with the beauty that comes from within, the unfading beauty of a gentle and quiet spirit, which is so precious to God." Living out this verse is true empowerment! So who are you? Do you know? Consider memorizing Psalm 139:14 (NLT) and repeat it to yourself often:

"Thank you for making me so wonderfully complex! Your workmanship is marvelous—how well I know it."

Your true worth is who God made you to be and how he made you. It's not centered around any mistakes you've made in your past. You are more than what you look like and what you do. You are more than any title another human can give to you. Before you are anybody's girlfriend, friend, wife, mother, sister, daughter, employee, etc., you are woman, made in God's image and precious to him. Let that soak in and feed your self-esteem and direct your actions! Press into who God made you to be. You have great worth, so live like it, and thank God for it.

I want to say here that part of being a woman is embracing your femininity. You may have had a father who either verbally or nonverbally let you know that he wished you had been born a son instead of a daughter. Perhaps you felt compelled to dress like a boy or wore your hair a certain way because you either consciously or unconsciously thought it would make your dad love and accept you more. This may have caused you to believe that you were not worthy or desired as a young girl, and these thoughts have followed you into adulthood, shaping your way of thinking and how you see yourself.

If this is you, I hope you will take some time to think through this in light of who your Heavenly Father made you to be and embrace it. Also, you can be authentic to your womanhood in any field or profession you've entered into, whether you're a stay-at-home mom, the CEO of a company, a ballerina, or a professional boxer like Laila Ali! In all that you do, be a woman. Don't compromise who you are. Thrive as a woman. That's who God made you to be!

Let your worth shape your actions and direct or redirect your decisions based on who God is and who he made you to be. Before I was married, I was in a negative cycle with my now-husband. We were having sex with each other; even though we were Christians, our actions didn't line up with what we knew God wanted for us. We knew better, but we continued in our sin. We knew sex before marriage was unwise and disobedient, but it wasn't until I embraced my worth and stood up for my own righteousness that this cycle of wrongdoing was broken. I began to understand that my worth was more valuable than anything or anyone else I was holding on to.

When I repented of my actions to God and valued my worth to the degree that I was willing to lose this relationship rather than continue doing something in it that was against God, a breakthrough happened. I confronted my partner and communicated my thoughts and worth to him, and he honored them. The cycle ended. Our relationship was the better for it, and we got married. That being said, a while after we were married, we experienced a rough patch and wondered what was going on. How come we weren't coming together as we had before? We realized we had to gain a new way of thinking and a new approach to loving and valuing each other now that it was legal! Sin can be exciting, but in the end, it destroys.

So, we did the hard work of examining ourselves, our relationship, and our past actions and gave it all to the Lord as a couple. Once we did, we felt worthy of living out our love. God restored our thinking, and we learned what marital love truly means, which is beautiful and authentic when it's between two people who know their worth in Christ.

Breaking Cycles

Do you find yourself in a negative cycle that you can't seem to break on your own? According to Merriam-Webster, a cycle is "a course or series of events or operations that recur regularly and usually lead back to the starting point." A cycle keeps us going in the same negative direction, never making a detour or a U-turn. It doesn't change. And the outcome is the same! This reminds me of a popular definition of insanity: "Doing the same thing over and over again and expecting different results." You may say, "Well, I'm doing things differently now!" But, if the outcome never changes, then you're actually doing things in the same old way.

For example, you may have a new boyfriend, but you soon find yourself in a similar situation with him as you had with the last boyfriend—new face but same 'ol cycle. Continue making the same poor decisions, like giving away your worth, and you will wake up and see that you're in the same place. There's really no difference. Or maybe you make fresh goals, but you're still procrastinating, still showing up late, still not being prepared, still not planning out the steps. Those new goals can be right on target, but if you're stuck in a cycle of not doing what you're supposed to, those wonderful goals will go unrealized . . . again.

When you surrender your life to God and trust him with it, he will help you break cycles that are harming you. Living in a negative cycle is a flashing red light telling you that you are compromising in some area or a number of areas in your life. When you compromise on God's Word, compromise on your worth, cycles are fueled and continue to exist. But when you decide to obey God and walk in his ways, you will begin to see cycles break down. You will be freed from them! You must take the Lord seriously. Can you identify any ways that you are currently giving in, making excuses, and rationalizing your behavior?

It's unwise to ignore negative cycles and fool yourself into thinking they will resolve themselves or just disappear. It's not true. It's essential that you forsake them and not allow them to rule. They require a choice of your will. A sobering verse that highlights this is found in the Old Testament.

"If you forsake the LORD and serve foreign gods, then He will turn and do you harm and consume you after He has done you good" (Joshua 24:2, NKJV).

When we find ourselves in negative cycles, and we don't address them but give them permission to continue, it's like we are serving foreign or false gods. The Bible tells us we will pay a high price for this. We must not go through life unaware of what we are doing! Pay attention; take notice, and when you're caught up in a negative cycle, choose to take steps to get rid of it.

The cycle you are in may be the result, in part, of the culture or the behavior surrounding you. But it's still up to you to put an end to it in your own life. You must invite God into the process and allow him to do the needed work in your life. He will help you to detach from the same old behavior, the same old reactions and ways of thinking and respond, think, and act in ways that are good for you and glorifying to him. Don't be like the Israelites who continually neglected to exercise their faith and, as a result, had to walk around and around in the wilderness for forty years!

Talk about a negative cycle! God rescued them out of bondage when they were slaves in Egypt, but they continued to want the old things instead of trusting God for the new life he had for them. This kept them in a type of cycle of bondage in the wilderness. If what they desired from God didn't come fast enough, they'd go right back to whining, complaining, panicking, and even wanting to go back to Egypt into the life of slavery they were living there! They didn't put their faith into action in their everyday lives, so they remained in a cycle of bondage though they were actually free. God did not allow that generation to see the Promised Land as a result.

You must trust God and walk in righteousness, so you are able to break strongholds (negative cycles) in your life. The situation I described to you earlier in the chapter illustrates this. I had to give up having sex before marriage—to repent of my actions and invite God into the process—in order to break free from the cycle. What have you allowed to attach itself to your soul that is unequally yoked with the Spirit of God? Identify it. Bring it out into the light. Acknowledge the cycle it has you in. This requires you to summon your courage and be willing to be honest with God and with yourself. Why would you want to remain tethered to a repeated cycle in your life that has created nothing but pain, misery, and guilt?

A cycle can be a false belief or way of thinking, emotional distress that we wallow in, the dysfunction we participate in with our relationships, being uncommitted to making progress in an area that needs action, any type of addiction, and so much more. When these things are habitual in our lives, a cycle is born that we must break.

Sometimes they can be a result of generational sin. If so, let these patterns end with you! Don't pass any of them on to your children. Instead, begin to deal with each negative cycle and get rid of it. Did your parents yell all the time, and now you find yourself yelling at your kids? Repent of that behavior and ask God to help you break this cycle, so it does not get passed on to the next generation and then the next. I remember, for instance, that I did not want to sleep around with different guys because I knew that was a pattern in my mom's life. It was a subtle thing for me as a kid, but I still knew it was going on; and I somehow knew that it was going to be an issue—a thorn in the flesh—in my life. It was something I had to constantly tell myself not to get trapped in, and yet it wasn't until I repented and stood up for myself and my worth with my future husband that I broke the cycle.

The Holy Spirit began the process when he convicted me. What is the Holy Spirit convicting you of? Pray and ask him. Prayer is also the key to putting an end to the cycle.

If you're ready to live free, ask God to help you form new, good habits and go in a new direction! Cycles are strong; you can't break them on your own. You may think you got rid of a cycle, but it comes back to visit to see if you'll allow it to take up residence again. Satan tempts, but God tests. How will you do? Prayer is essential. It will fortify you. Talk to God and reclaim and proclaim who you are in Christ. Ask God to help you identify harmful cycles and have the resolve and strength to break them. Then ask him to help you form healthy habits in their place. He can help you to be disciplined, focused, self-aware, etc.

This will change your trajectory. You will move forward in the right way and in the right direction. When the cycle or cycles are broken for good, you will begin to obtain your goals, expand your vision, and you will be in a better emotional state of mind. You can say, for example, "I don't have to be broke this January like I was last January. I can spend less and exercise self-control." And then move forward to make that your reality by planning and asking for God's help.

You will also have a closer relationship with your Heavenly Father when you are allowing him to break old habits and cycles. When you see the cycles dissolving, it means that your worship has changed; your obedience to him has changed. You're probably spending more time in the Word, and you're being careful to fellowship with God's people. Keeping good company helps you in the process as others encourage you to maintain good habits and break negative cycles. Then, you are a better example to your family and others.

As women, especially, we can shift an environment in a big way. Of course, anyone can influence their environment for good or bad, but women are often a little more emotionally defined. We need to be careful. Our emotions fuel our attitude and actions, and that affects others! So, commit to breaking the bondage of generational and willful sin, and begin to model a righteous life that inspires change for those you have influence over. You will see and enjoy the fruit of healthy habits in your own life and be able to live out your womanhood in its fullness.

Unconditional Love

When women come to my office to meet with me, a common topic we discuss is *love*. Love for themselves, love for others, the absence of love, their struggle with love, and more. How you experience love is a foundational part of how you are shaped and how you see and treat yourself and others. There are many forms or "flavors" of love, but unconditional love is not only the most desired but the most needed. And it's found in God. We experience unconditional love when we have an encounter with Jesus Christ. In him alone, perfect, unconditional love is found.

So what is unconditional love? Merriam-Webster defines "unconditional" as "not conditional or limited: absolute, unqualified." That definition is straightforward, but the word "love" is more complicated to define.

Although psychologists often cite seven types of love, we see that there are three main types of love defined in the Bible: Philos, Eros, and Agape.

First, let's look briefly at phileo or philos love. This is the love we share in friendship. It's the love we have for our fellow man and woman; it's warm and compassionate. Philadelphia is called the "City of Brotherly Love." Phileo is not usually as emotionally intense as romantic or "eros" love, but at its core is devotion and affection. In the Bible, we see this love between David and Jonathan. "And Jonathan and David made a covenant together because Jonathan loved David as much as himself" (1 Samuel 18:3, AMP). These two men were devoted to one another in their friendship. They loved each other with a strong phileo love. We're given a straightforward command to love this way in Romans 12:10: "Be devoted to one another in love. Honor one another above yourselves."

Do you have this type of love in your life? Do you give it to others? Love is, after all, an action word. It's more than a feeling.

The second type of love is eros. This love is to be experienced within the context of marriage. It's an intimate, romantic, erotic, or sexual love. The world often distorts and pollutes what eros is really all about. It turns it into something that is not truly love but lust and calls it "love." But true eros love is beautiful and a gift from God, yet a marriage won't last on this passionate love alone. Partnered with philos love in a marriage, eros love is enhanced in a sustaining way. God's Word doesn't shy away from addressing eros love. 1 Corinthians 7:3 says, "The husband should fulfill his wife's sexual needs, and the wife should fulfill her husband's needs." And in the book of Song of Solomon, we read, "Kiss me, and kiss me again, for your love is sweeter than wine."

The Word of God is clear—eros love is from God and to be lived out and enjoyed in our marital relationship.

The third type of love we are wise to embrace is agape. This is God's unconditional love for us. It's also his love for his son, Jesus. And it's the umbrella over all other types of love and demonstrates how God wants us to love others. You can't experience this love in its purest form unless you have a relationship with Jesus Christ. The amazing news is God has initiated agape love with you, and you just need to accept it!

> "But God is so rich in mercy, and he loved us so much that even though we were dead because of our sins, he gave us life when he raised Christ from the dead. [It is only by God's grace that you have been saved!]" (Ephesians 2:4–5 AMP).

We're told in 1 John 4:9–10: "In this, the love of God was made manifest among us, that God sent his only son into the world so that we might live through him. In this is love, not that we loved God but that he loved us." The truth of unconditional love affects how we see ourselves and how we love others. It should cause us to praise and worship God! Do you know what a life-changing gift unconditional love is? It's found in all its glory in Christ alone. God doesn't change his love for you even when you are not acting in an ideal way. His love is perfect, pure, and never changing.

Agape love is always unconditional. It's also the key to living an abundant life. In all our struggles and challenges, in the midst of engaging in self-sabotaging behavior, and as we fight against harmful cycles and seek to break them, we are given the power we need to overcome, succeed, and love others. These things are made possible through God's love for us. So, when you accept and rely on his unconditional love, power is unleashed.

"We know how much God loves us, and we have put our trust in his love. God is love, and all who live in love live in God, and God lives in them. And as we live in God, our love grows more perfect" (1 John 4:16–17b, NLT).

The New International Version says, "... we know and rely on the love God has for us ..." Being dependent upon this love and offering it to others ushers in a life that is worth celebrating.

Examine your relationships. Is your love for others conditional? I remember struggling in a few relationships I had with men. I felt like I gave the person my all, and then they disappointed me or even broke my heart. After being wounded, I learned to put up barriers and set up conditions. I would think to myself, *if he does this for me, then I'll do that for him.* We can think the same way about our friendships. "I bought her a birthday gift, so I expect her to buy me a birthday gift!"

If we're honest, sometimes we unconditionally love our pets more than we do our fellow humans! Many of us go out of our way for them without complaint. We give and give to our cats and dogs without restrictions, expectations, and conditions. That's not wrong, but shouldn't we at least give the people in our lives the same consideration and unconditional love?

Now, examine your love for yourself. If you reject yourself or put conditions on your love and you stop seeing yourself as God sees you, you will not value your worth. You may experience and live out of self-hate. You will engage in self-sabotaging behavior, fall into dysfunctional relationships, and live in or be motivated by fear. Fear is not a part of God's unconditional love.

"Such love has no fear because perfect love expels all fear. If we are afraid, it is for fear of punishment, and this shows that we have not fully experienced his perfect love" (1 John 4:8, NLT).

His unconditional love accepts you as you are—even when you are at your worst—and empowers you. It's what you need to be whole and victorious, and it's yours through Christ. The Bible also tells us that nothing can separate you from God's love. It's unconditional and unending. And, though we operate in these different types of love throughout our lives, it's agape love we must cling to above all else. When you navigate life with unconditional love as your goal, you will be a blessing to others and experience blessings yourself.

Remember, God puts no limitations on his love for you! Of course, you can't love perfectly, but you can look to Jesus and ask the Holy Spirit to help you love yourself and love others with agape love. If you are not praying and submitting to the will of God and the purpose he has for your life, you can't love unconditionally. You will put conditions on your love for yourself and others. So, when you understand who you are as a woman—as God's woman, his daughter—and that you are fully, unconditionally loved, you will see yourself and others with his eyes, and you will desire to love in that way. Only the sovereign grace and love of God can prompt that desire.

Still, I must warn you that when you set out to love unconditionally, roadblocks will inevitably get in the way. Conditions will wiggle their way in, so be aware, guard your thinking, and make a choice (over and over again) to love unconditionally.

One wonderful resource I recommend to give you insight on how we generally want to give and receive love is found in a book called *The Five Love Languages* by Gary Chapman. In it, he talks about five actions that convey love: Words of affirmation, quality time, gifts, acts of service, and physical touch. Being aware of how your loved ones want to be loved and recognizing what speaks love to you (and then expressing that to significant people in your life so they can know) will enhance your relationships.

Additionally, take some time to dwell on the beautiful attributes of love we are given in 1 Corinthians 13:4–7 (NLT):

"Love is patient and kind. Love is not jealous or boastful or proud, or rude. It does not demand its own way. It is not irritable, and it keeps no record of being wronged. It does not rejoice about injustice but rejoices whenever the truth wins out. Love never gives up, never loses faith, is always hopeful, and endures through every circumstance."

The Redemption

The greatest demonstration of God's love is when he made a way for us to be in a forever relationship with him. This happened when he redeemed us by his son, Jesus. Redemption may sound like an old-fashioned word, but it is certainly relevant today and always will be.

The common definition of redemption is "the act of making something better or more acceptable" (Merriam-Webster). But the biblical definition by that same source as it applies to Christianity is "the act of saving people from sin and evil" and "the fact of being saved from sin or evil." When you come to Christ aware of your sin, repent of it (admit it and turn from it), and accept God's love by inviting Jesus to be your Savior, you are redeemed. Period.

At the end of the day, redemption reconciles us to a place of full acceptance in Christ. Ephesians 1:7 (NLT) says, "He is so rich in kindness and grace that he purchased our freedom with the blood of his son and forgave our sins." When you're redeemed, you have been saved from the penalty of sin. You are forever forgiven. You've been restored to a place of right standing with your Heavenly Father. That ought to make you dance for joy and sing praises to the Lord!

If you have accepted Christ, I want to challenge you as a woman of God to fully embrace that you have been redeemed and forgiven. You have the power of the Holy Spirit to love God, yourself, and others. You can know and understand that you have God's protection. Your life is worth living and celebrating, so you must guard against destroying your life. Remind yourself that you are saved, and with that, you have forgiveness and now protection.

You don't have to sabotage your life with negative words or behaviors or give in to feelings of unworthiness. You can chase those feelings away when they surface because of God's redemption and restoration in your life. He has so much more for you than living under strongholds. You no longer have to live under an unrealistic standard of perfection that the world demands in order for you to be "OK." You have freedom in Christ, and it's only in him that you are being made perfect.

" . . . He who began a good work in you will perfect it until the day of Christ Jesus" (Philippians 1:6, NASB).

So you don't have to compromise, settle, or become something you were never intended to be. Instead, live out of his unconditional love. Live out the Fruit of the Spirit—love, joy, peace, patience, kindness, goodness, faithfulness, gentleness, and self-control.

Whatever your life looks like at this moment, whatever your circumstances are, there is redemption. Redemption is going on, and it's ongoing! He redeems our pain, our heartache, our mistakes. There is no situation you can experience that God can't redeem. When my first husband and I were divorcing, I felt like I was falling back into a place of being a single mom, which I dreaded, but God redeemed that situation. I ended up getting remarried to a wonderful man, but even if I hadn't, God's redemption work was taking place in my life and in the lives of my children. I still had a loving, kind Heavenly Father who was fathering my children.

Are you unmarried but longing for a husband? Before you are anyone's wife, you belong to God. You are married to him! Jesus is referred to in the Bible as the Bridegroom, and you are his bride.

Accept and embrace his gift of redemption in all areas of your life. No one is good enough, smart enough, or clever enough to provide their own lasting redemption. You can try and make things right on your own, but it won't last. But when you do things through the Spirit of God, letting his Spirit lead you, there is genuine redemption for every circumstance. Walking in the Spirit is a lifestyle. This is how you live out your redemption on a day-to-day basis. No matter what is going on in your life, no matter what mistakes you make, the shame and guilt you struggle with, even your own pride that gets in the way, redemption is yours. Redemption provides safety and assurance no matter what you're experiencing at this moment, what you've experienced in the past, and what you will experience in the future.

Redemption is all about forgiveness. God forgave and continues to forgive. You have been showered with forgiveness, and in order for you to be able to experience it in all its fullness, you must extend that forgiveness to others. Don't fall into the dangerous mindset of thinking that you are entitled to something that you are not willing to give to someone else. You will find yourself in a place of healing and wholeness as you let go of offenses against you and forgive the offender(s).

One tool I use in my practice to help women get to a place of forgiveness is an exercise called forgiveness therapy. Forgiveness is about a decision to overcome the pain that was inflicted by another person. It requires being willing to let go of everything you have gone through, challenged by, etc., so you can get into the mindset of redemption. Forgiveness is not necessarily reconciling with another person and returning to that relationship if it has been severed, but it is pardoning that person. Yet when you go the extra mile, forgiveness can be reparative.

If you've been hurt by your mom, for example, and you forgive her, chances are the relationship will be repaired (at least to a degree) when your forgiveness is put into action. When you are kind, patient, and gentle, for example, you are enacting unconditional love, and repairing the relationship is possible. It should help to remember that the Bible says your own sins have been removed and will never be brought back again. They are gone, forgotten.

"He has removed our sins as far from us as the east is from the west" (Psalm 103:12, NLT).

So, dear woman, live in forgiveness. Live in the freedom of knowing that you have been fully forgiven, and there's freedom in granting forgiveness to others. When you do, you will move forward in victory and wholeness. You will live in a way worthy of your redemption.

Keys to Remember

I hope you've found these chapters to be helpful. I've done my job if it has unlocked for you a few "truth treasures" so that you now have a better understanding regarding some issues in your life. Once you understand who you are as a woman and that you may not have always been protected by the people you had hoped to be protected by and that, as a result, perhaps sabotaging has been taking place (either by our own doing or by the actions of others), you will begin to change. Your life will be different. You will no longer give away your worth, and you will be able to begin to break cycles that have held you down.

I hope this book has whet your appetite to dig in even deeper with any issues it has uncovered for you, and I pray you feel compelled now to take these valuable keys to remember and use them to unlock the tools needed to adjust, tweak, and straighten out some things! However, none of this is possible in a life-changing way other than through the power and love of Jesus Christ. You must repent of your sins and accept his unconditional love for you in order to experience a redeemed life that frees you to live in forgiveness, love, and wholeness. That's it in a nutshell!

So, hey, woman! From the heart of this counselor... Rely on God. Trust in his love. Keep talking about it and working things through! Learn and put that knowledge and insight into action.

I want you to live a life worth celebrating, but more importantly, that's what your Creator wants for you. He's given you his unconditional love to empower you and has provided the Holy Spirit to assist you. Remember, too, that there is no shame in seeking additional help. God uses mental health counseling (such as cognitive behavioral therapy) along with his Word to help us be the people he made us to be.

By blending the biblical and therapeutic approach, a trained counselor can help you uncover your true potential, leading you to your best life, no matter your past experiences. It takes some work and time, but it's an investment worth making.